Postman Pat
and the
Christmas Post

It was nearly Christmas and there was deep snow in Greendale. Each day, Pat had more and more Christmas parcels and letters to deliver. Jess had to curl up small to make room for them.

"I've never known such a busy Christmas," said Pat.

Everyone in Greendale was busy getting ready for Christmas. Granny Dryden was busy knitting warm woolly jumpers for all her friends and relations. Ted Glen was busy making wooden trucks and trains.

Alf Thompson was busy making walking-sticks from sheep's horn. Miss Hubbard was busy making beetroot wine, and table-mats, and calendars. Mrs. Pottage was busy making poker-work pictures. The Reverend Timms was busy making framed pictures of Greendale Church. Katy and Tom were busy making all kinds of pictures and presents and decorations, at home and at school.

Everyone was busy writing Christmas cards.

And when all these cards and presents had been addressed, and wrapped up, and tied up, and stuck together with sticky-tape, they had to go in the post. When Pat emptied the letter-boxes, they were full to bursting.

Postman Pat's
Winter Storybook

Postman Pat's
Winter Storybook

by John Cunliffe
Illustrated by Celia Berridge
from the original Television designs by Ivor Wood

Hippo Books
Scholastic Publications Limited
London

Scholastic Publications Ltd.,
10 Earlham Street, London WC2H 9RX, UK

Scholastic Inc.,
730 Broadway, New York, NY 10003, USA

Scholastic Tab Publications Ltd.,
123 Newkirk Road, Richmond Hill,
Ontario L4C 3G5, Canada

Ashton Scholastic Pty. Ltd.,
PO Box 579, Gosford, New South Wales,
Australia

Ashton Scholastic Ltd.,
165 Marua Road, Panmure, Auckland 6,
New Zealand

First published in the UK
by André Deutsch Limited 1987

This edition published by
Scholastic Publications Ltd., 1989

Text copyright © John Cunliffe 1987
Illustration copyright © Celia Berridge
and Woodland Animations Limited

ISBN 0 590 76127 7

Made and printed in Belgium by Proost
International Bookproduction

10 9 8 7 6 5 4 3 2 1

Contents

Every day, the post-office was full of people, buying stamps, and cards, and string, and sticky-tape, and wrapping-paper, and envelopes; weighing their parcels, and asking for more stamps, and air-mail labels; asking how much it would be to send a parcel to France, or America, or Africa. Poor Mrs. Goggins was run off her feet.

"I'm glad Christmas is only once a year," she said.

Then, one cold and frosty morning, Pat had a surprise when he walked into the post-office. Mrs. Goggins was smiling.

"I have a helper, now," she said.

"Who can it be?" said Pat.

He could hear someone in the back room, busy sorting the parcels, and singing to himself. "I'm sure I know that voice," said Pat, "but I just can't place it."

"You'll never guess," said Mrs. Goggins. "Have a look, and see."

"Well, I never!" said Pat.

It was Ted Glen. He was wearing a special post-office badge, to show that he was a proper post-office Christmas post worker.

"Hello, Pat," said Ted. "How am I doing?"

"You look to be doing a good job, as far as I can see," said Pat.

"I'll give you a hand with the village post," said Ted, "so you can get on with the farms. You'd better get round to them before this snow gets too deep."

"Thanks, Ted," said Pat. "I'll be glad of some help."

Ted set out with a big bag of letters and parcels for the houses of the village.

"One thing," he said, "it gets lighter as you go along. Cheerio!"

Ted was on his way, and Pat soon followed with a van full of Christmas post.

There was a wonderful welcome at each house and farm that Pat called at. They had hot drinks and mince pies ready for him, and presents wrapped in shiny paper, with labels saying, "NOT TO BE OPENED UNTIL 25TH DECEMBER". There were saucers of cream and toy mice for Jess.

"We'll be too full to eat our dinner," said Pat.

The snow went on falling, day after day. Pat was going up the hill to Thompson Ground when his front wheels slipped on the ice, and the whole van skated across the road and into a deep ditch. Now Pat was well and truly stuck.

"What are we going to do now, Jess?" he said. "If we don't get round with these parcels, half the people of Green-dale won't get their Christmas presents in time. It's going to be cold waiting for help, too. We'll just have to lock up and walk up the hill to see if Alf can bring his tractor down to pull us out."

Just as Pat was setting out on the long walk, there was the sound of another engine coming up the hill. It was Sam, in his mobile shop. He stopped when he saw Pat's van. It wasn't Sam's usual day for visiting Greendale, so Pat was surprised to see him.

"Hello," said Pat, "what are you doing up this way today?"

"It's a special trip," said Sam. "Look in my van and you'll see why."

"Good gracious!" said Pat. Sam's van had none of its usual groceries in it. He had taken the shelves out, and there was a pile of parcels instead.

"I have a post-office badge, like Ted's," said Sam. "I've hired my van to the post-office, to help with the Christmas post. And it looks as though you're stuck, with a load of parcels still to deliver."

"Yes," said Pat, "and it's getting late. It'll be dark soon, and this snow's getting bad."

"I'll take a share of your parcels," said Sam. "You stay here, and I'll go back and ask Peter Fogg to bring the big tractor to pull you out. He'll be here in a jiffy."

"Thanks," said Pat. "What a good thing you came along."

They shared the parcels out, and Sam went back down the hill. Pat and Jess didn't have long to wait. They were very glad to hear the roar of Peter's engine coming up the hill. Peter soon pulled Pat's van out of the ditch. Then he did better than that. He had his snow-plough fitted to the front of the tractor, so he drove in front of Pat, clearing a way through the snow. Alf and Dorothy Thompson were delighted to see them. They thought they were snowed-in for the week.

"If you hadn't come," said Alf, "we'd have had no parcels, no cards, and no visitors, all Christmas. Bless you, both."

Pat and Peter couldn't stop; they had to push on before snow and darkness stopped them. Peter went ahead, up all the hill roads, and cleared the snow. Pat followed as fast he could, with the post.

When, at last, they got back to the village, and the safety and shelter of the valley, they were cold and tired. Mrs. Goggins had hot drinks and Christmas cake waiting for them in her sitting-room behind the post-office, and they sat in front of a big fire to warm their toes. Sam and Ted soon came in to join them. Ted's post-bag was empty, and so was Sam's van, but there was a load of parcels for Sam to take to Pencaster to catch the evening post and the train to London.

"Oh, Pat," said Mrs. Goggins, "I mustn't forget to tell you; there was a phone call from the vicarage. The Reverend said would you please be sure to call at the village hall on your way home tonight. Now you won't forget will you? He said it was important."

"I'll not forget," said Pat.

It was time for everyone to go their different ways. They wished each other "Safe journey!" and "Merry Christmas!" and they were all on their way.

Pat remembered to call at the village hall. And what a scene he saw there! He walked into the middle of the village-institute Christmas party for all the Greendale children. And, who do you think was sitting by the Christmas Tree, giving out presents to the children? Father Christmas himself! Pat said he wished he could have a flying-sleigh, drawn by reindeer, to deliver his parcels, and that made Father Christmas laugh. He had a special present for Jess; a small parcel, done up in blue ribbon.

"I wonder what it can be," said Pat. "Now Jess will have a parcel to open on Christmas Day."

Pat joined in a dance with the children, and kissed Miss Hubbard under the mistletoe. Jess gave Lucy Selby a kiss; a lick on the nose. Then it was time for Pat to be on his way home.

Christmas Eve soon came. It was time to put out the post-office lights and lock up for the holiday. Mrs. Goggins was looking forward to a good rest after all the extra work. Everyone was!

All the cards and parcels had been delivered, and everything was ready for the excitements of Christmas Day itself. The children of Greendale could think of nothing but the moment when Father Christmas would call. Of wakening up very early in the morning, to find a stocking filled with presents at the foot of the bed. Of sitting round the Christmas tree, with a pile of exciting parcels waiting to be opened. Oh, how would the minutes between now and then ever pass?

But they did pass. Very early in the morning, on Christmas Day, lights began to wink on in cottages and farms, wherever children lived, the whole length of Greendale. In Pat's house, young Julian woke Pat and Sara by jumping on their bed with his loaded stocking. He snuggled in between them, to pull his presents out one by one. Then it was out of bed and down to the tree, to see the parcels waiting there. Pat was far too sleepy to open his presents, until he had made a cup of tea. As for Jess, when he saw that it was still dark, he curled up in his basket and went back to sleep.

They had a lovely Christmas, and Pat had three whole days with no letters or parcels to deliver. They went to church for the Reverend Timms' Christmas Day service. Miss Hubbard conducted the choir, who sang beautifully, and Peter Fogg pumped the organ. On Boxing Day, they went to the pantomime in the village hall; it was "Jack and the Beanstalk" this year. On the day after Boxing Day, Jess decided to open his present. He tore it open with his claws, when no one was looking.

Then he carried it off in his mouth and hid it somewhere. I wonder what it was?

Snowman
Postman

In the middle of January it became still colder in Greendale. More snow fell. It began to melt; there was some rain; then it froze again. It froze so hard that everything had a coat of ice. When Pat got up in the morning, he could not open the door of his van.

He chipped at the ice with a kitchen-knife, but he still couldn't get his key into the lock. He poured warm water over the lock and over the windows; it still wouldn't open. He held a candle so that its flame licked round the lock. Now the key would go in, but it wouldn't turn. He warmed his key on the stove in the kitchen, until it was nearly too hot to hold. Then, it turned in the lock and opened the door.

Pat was on his way, at last, but, oh, it was so cold! Jess fluffed his fur up, and Pat wore his thickest scarf and gloves.

On the way, they saw Ted Glen. He was busy chopping wood. He had no gloves and no scarf on! Pat stopped for a chat. "Aren't you cold?" he said.

"Not a bit," said Ted. "There's nothing like a bit of chopping to warm you up."

At Greendale Farm, Peter Fogg was breaking the ice on the trough so that the cows could have a drink.

"I bet they'd rather have a warm cup of tea," said Pat.

"I don't know what their milk would taste like," said Peter," if we gave them tea to drink."

Katy and Tom came running across the stack-yard.

"You're too late, Pat," said Katy. "Our postman's already here."

"Come and see," said Tom.

They took him round the corner by the barn. There stood a snowman postman. He had coal-eyes and mouth, a carrot-nose, an old scarf round his neck, and a bag for his letters.

"Poor fellow," said Pat. "He has no hat. He'll get a cold head. He can borrow mine, but only for a minute." He put his hat on the snowman's head. Now he looked much more like a real postman.

The twins filled his bag with snowballs, and Pat made him a snow-parcel. Large flakes of snow began to fall from the sky.

"Here come some more letters," said Pat. "I hope he gets them all delivered. I can't see any addresses on them. Now don't forget to make him a snow-Jess, and a hat as well. I must be on my way, and I'd be too cold without my hat."

"I'm going to make him a snow-van," said Tom.

"No, an ice-van," said Pat. "That's what mine was this morning."

Pat took the letters in to Mrs. Pottage, then went on his way.

At Thompson Ground, young Bill was making a giant snowball. He had started with a small one. Then he had rolled it round and round on the grass. It grew bigger and bigger, until it was so big that he couldn't move it. Pat gave him an extra push with it. It rolled down the hill, picking up still more snow, and growing bigger. It hit the wall at the bottom and broke into pieces. There was a glove sticking out of one piece.

"So that's where my glove went to," said Bill. "That was a piece of luck. I thought I was going to get into trouble for losing that."

When Pat had delivered all his letters and parcels, he was glad to get home to his warm fireside. There was soon a good meal on the table, then it was time for Pat, and Sara, and young Julian, to watch their favourite television programmes. Jess curled up by the fire, too, and had a cat nap; but, after the News, Jess woke up, walked slowly across the room, mewed, and scratched at the door.

"He wants to go out," said Sara.

"Nay, Jess," said Pat. "You don't want to go out in this weather, do you?"

But Jess did want to go out. He scratched and scratched at the door until Pat opened it. A cold blast of air blew in.

"Brrrrr," said Pat. "Don't be long, Jess. It's cold enough to freeze your tail off." Jess ran down the garden path, into the darkness.

Where was he going? Perhaps to see if the mice had come out of their holes, in the barn at Greendale Farm? Wherever it was, he meant to get there, snow or no snow.

Julian went off to bed, and Pat read him a chapter from his favourite Moomin book. When Pat came downstairs again, Sara said, "Jess hasn't come back. I've just been out to look, and there's no sign of him in the garden. It's snowing hard, too. I do hope he's all right."

"The wind's getting up as well," said Pat. "There'll be drifts by morning; it could get really deep. But I expect Jess's in someone's barn, hunting mice. If it's too cold to come home, he'll find a warm bit of hay to curl up in for the night."

Jess didn't come home that night. The next day, the snow was very deep, and Pat couldn't get his van out until the snow-plough had been along the road. They were all very worried about Jess; there was still no sign of him.

"I'll look in all the barns as I go on my rounds," said Pat, "and ask if anyone's seen him. Somebody's sure to have spotted him. Every-one knows Jess in Greendale."

The snow was deep everywhere, and the wind had piled it up into deep drifts in the fields. Pat kept asking about Jess, but no one had seen him. He looked in all the barns, but there was no sign of Jess anywhere. When he called at Thompson Ground, Alf was just setting out to look for some of his sheep; they were lost in the snow, and they would soon die if they didn't get some food.

"I wonder if your Jess's under a snowdrift, like my sheep," said Alf.

All the farmers knew how the sheep could make a space under the snow, like a little snow-house, and be quite safe in it, for a time. They would huddle together to keep warm, and the walls of snow would keep the cold wind off them. But they had no food under the snow, so the farmers had to find them quickly.

"I'll come and give you a hand, looking for your sheep," said Pat. "I can't deliver any more letters until the snow-plough gets up here. That top road's sure to be blocked."

"Right," said Alf. "Thanks, Pat. Let's get going, then."

They took one of the farm-dogs, Floss, to help sniff out the sheep. They also took a long thin rod and a spade each. The snow was frozen hard, and they could walk on the top of the drifts, without sinking in. The snow was so deep that you could walk right over the tops of the walls. Up the hillside they went. The icy wind blew, and made their noses and cheeks sting. When they came to a place where Alf thought the sheep might be they stopped, whilst Floss ran about sniffing and snuffling at the snow, pushing her nose into any hole or crack or cranny, by walls and trees where the sheep might have sheltered. Then Alf and Pat gently pushed their long rods down into the snowdrifts, feeling for the snow-cave the sheep could have made.

They tried four deep drifts in this way, but they had no luck. They were just going to turn back to the farm, when Pat said, "What about the old barn in the bottom meadow? They might have gone there for shelter, then been snowed in."

"There's just a chance," said Alf. "We'll have a look there, then we'll go home for a hot mug of tea. I think we've earned it."

The old barn had no roof; it had blown off one windy day that Pat remembered only too well. They tramped across the snow. They were getting tired and cold. Just one more place to look, then they could go and get warm.

The walls of the old barn were open to the snow and to the wind. The snow had blown in, and piled up inside just as deep as it was outside. Floss sniffed and wagged her tail.

"I think she's smelt something," said Alf, "but it might only be a fox." Floss's tail went faster and faster.

"She's certainly found something," Alf went on. "Let's try the rods."

Alf and Pat carefully pushed their rods into the deep snow. Down and down, as far as they could reach. Pat's rod felt different. One moment, he was pushing the rod through the snow, then it went more easily. Perhaps it had come to a space under the snow. Perhaps it had come to the snow-cave made by the warm bodies of the sheep?

"Come and try here," said Pat. "I think I can feel something."

Alf came to try in Pat's place. Yes. Yes. It was the same with Alf's rod.

"I think we've found something," said Alf. "We'd better dig it out, and have a look."

They dug down into the drift. It was hard work, but it made them warm. Floss ran about in the snow, yelping with excitement. Far down, under the snow, in a corner by the wall, Pat uncovered a hole in the snow. They stopped digging. A woolly nose came to the little gap, and sniffed.

"Thank goodness," said Alf, "we've found them!"

They had to dig more slowly and carefully, now. They didn't want to hurt the sheep with the sharp spades. They made the hole bigger and bigger, until it was big enough to get the sheep out. They could see more and more woolly bodies cuddled together under the snow, and they could feel how warm they were. The sheep didn't want to come out; it was warmer under the snow than it was out in the cold wind. Alf had to pull them out, one by one.

"There must be about ten of them in there," said Alf.

But Alf and Pat were very surprised when they saw what else was in there with the sheep, keeping warm amongst their woolly coats. There was a small black and white shape there, and it uncurled and ran to Pat when it saw him!

"Jess!" said Pat. "It's my Jess! Dear little Jess, whatever are you doing here, under the snow? Are you all right, Jess?"

He picked Jess up, and tucked him inside his warm overcoat. "Well, I never," he said.

Jess began to purr. He snuggled under Pat's coat, with just his nose peeping out. He soon felt as warm as toast.

"I wonder how you got here, with Alf's sheep?" said Pat. "I wonder."

But Jess couldn't tell him, so Pat never found out.

Pat and Alf went back to the farm to get some bales of hay for the sheep. Pat left Jess by the fire, and Dorothy gave him a saucer of milk. My goodness, how he purred. He almost purred his head off.

Pat and Alf came back to warm themselves by the fire, and have a good hot drink. They felt like purring, too; it was so good to be warm again.

Later, Alf would go with the tractor to bring the sheep back to the farm. As they sat there, they heard something climbing the hill, and going on past the farm, with its diesel engine at full power, and a shwooshing sound going with it.

"That sounds like the snow-plough," said Pat. "I expect Peter Fogg's driving it. That means I can get on with these letters. I'd better be on my way."

"Thanks for helping with the sheep," said Alf.

"Thanks for helping me to find Jess," said Pat. "Cheerio!"

It was a long, cold, journey for Pat that day, round all the frozen farms and cottages. Jess stayed curled up in his warm basket.

When Pat was on his way home, he called in at Greendale Farm, to see how the postman-snowman was getting on. There was no sign of him. He was buried under a huge drift of snow.

"Poor fellow," said Pat. "I hope he has some snow-sheep to keep him warm under there."

Then it was time to go home.

That night, Jess stayed by the fireside. He didn't scratch at the door; not once.

Postman Pat
Goes Fishing

The weather was much better in Greendale. The snow had gone, and it was much warmer.

"I reckon the winter's past its worst," said Pat to Mrs. Goggins, one Tuesday morning.

"Yes," said Mrs. Goggins. "I'm glad it's better. It's the children's half-term holiday this week; they'll be able to get out a bit and play outside."

"But there's quite a wind blowing," said Pat. "Hello, who's this big parcel for? Mrs. Thompson? Ah, she's been waiting for that. It'll be her new dress from that mail-order place in Manchester."

"She'll want it for the church-outing," said Mrs. Goggins. "She'll be glad it's come in time."

"Well," said Pat, "there's a good load of post today. I'd better be off. Cheerio!"

And Pat was on his way.

At Greendale Farm, Katy and Tom were playing with their new kite. It flew high in the sky, swooping and swerving from side to side as the wind buffeted it.

"That's just the thing for a windy day like this," said Pat. "Do you know how to send a letter to your kite?"

They didn't know, so Pat showed them.

Mrs. Pottage had opened her letters. "Don't throw that old envelope away," said Pat. "Do you mind if we use it to send a letter to the kite?"

She laughed, and looked puzzled, but she gave Pat the envelope.

"Now, this is how you do it," said Pat.

He made a hole in the middle of the envelope, and tore a slit from the hole to the edge. Then he threaded the envelope on to the kite-string. He pushed it a little way up the string. Then the wind caught it. It went sliding up the string at a good speed. The higher it went, the more wind it caught, and the faster it went. Up and up, higher than the houses, higher than the trees, it went. Half way up the string, it stopped.

"Oh, there's a knot in the string," said Katy. "It's stuck on the knot. Now Mrs. Kite won't get her letter."

"Oh, yes she will," said Pat. "I always deliver my letters properly."

He gave the string a shake, and a twitch, and another shake. The letter jumped over the knot, and went on, whizzing up the string. It went right up to the kite, and there it had to stop.

"Special delivery," said Pat. "On time, as always."

But now the wind changed direction. The kite did a nose-dive.
"Oh," shouted Tom, "it's going to crash!"

The kite crashed into a tree, far up the hillside, two fields away.
Katy and Tom began to cry.

"Don't cry," said Pat. "I'll get it for you." He sprinted across the
field. Mrs. Pottage had gone in to do the washing-up, and Pat didn't
hear her calling to him from the kitchen window.

"Pat! Look out! Don't go in the top meadow!"

She was trying to tell him what
was in the top meadow. Something
Pat would not want to find! He
found the kite. He had to climb up
into the tree to get it. He took no
notice of the herd of cows, eating the
grass at the far side of the field. He
just climbed up into the tree to get
the kite.

But, when he was climbing down again, he noticed that the cows had come much nearer. He was just going to jump down to the ground, when he saw, standing amongst the cows, a large bull! It had a ring in its nose. It was very large, and it had sharp horns. It stood looking at him. Pat thought he had better stay in the tree. Even better, he climbed a little higher up. Pat sat in the tree, and watched the bull. The bull stood on the grass, and watched Pat. They could very well stay there all day, looking at each other. Whatever was Pat going to do?

"I'm certainly not coming down, whilst he's there," said Pat to himself.

It was lucky for Pat that Mrs. Pottage knew where he had gone. She ran across the yard to Peter Fogg; he was busy washing the tractor. She said something very quickly to Peter, and in a few minutes, Pat heard the tractor starting up, and roaring across the fields towards him. He had never been so glad to see Peter and his tractor. Poor Pat. His hands and legs were getting stiff, and he feared that he was going to fall out of the tree. Then the bull could do what it liked with him.

Peter couldn't help laughing at the sight of Pat, stuck in the tree, with the bull staring up at him. But he soon sorted things out.

Peter didn't seem at all scared of the bull. He stopped the tractor nearby. Then he jumped down, walked up to the bull, raised his arms in the air, and shouted, "Hup, boy! Get up then! Get up!"

The bull turned slowly, and walked off. When it was a good distance away, Pat climbed down from the tree, with the kite.

"Oh, thank you," he said to Peter. "Thank you so much. I was really scared of your bull."

"You're welcome," said Peter. "It's no trouble. Jump up behind."

Pat climbed on the back of the tractor, and Peter drove back to the farmhouse.

"Come and have a cup of tea," said Mrs. Pottage. "I'm sorry you had such a fright from our old bull. I shouted to warn you, but you were in such a hurry that you didn't hear me."

"I feel a bit silly, now," said Pat. "Peter wasn't scared of the bull at all."

"Oh, but you were right to stay up the tree," said Mrs. Pottage. "That bull knows Peter, but there's no telling how he'd be with a stranger. They're dangerous things, bulls. You keep away from them."

"I will," said Pat. "I didn't know kite-flying could be so exciting."

Pat's next call was at Thompson Ground. Dorothy Thompson came out to meet him.

"Your parcel's come," said Pat. "The one you were waiting for."

"Oh, my new dress," said Dorothy, "oh, good, I am glad it's come."

"Would you just sign for it, please," said Pat, "in my book?"

"Yes, of course," said Dorothy. "May I borrow your pen, Pat?"

Pat handed her his pen. She looked round for somewhere to put the parcel whilst she signed. They were standing near the well in the farmyard, so she popped it there, on the wall by the well. She signed the book and gave it to Pat. Then what happened next? Afterwards, neither Pat nor Dorothy could be sure. Was it a gust of wind, that came round the corner and tipped the parcel into the well? Did Dorothy's skirt catch it as she turned back towards Pat? It was very hard to tell. What was sure, was that the parcel fell down the well with a splash!

"Oh, my dress! My new dress!" said Dorothy. "It's gone down the well!"

"Don't worry," said Pat. "I'm sure I can get it out for you, some-how."

"Get it out!" shouted Dorothy. "What's the use of getting it out, when it's been in that muddy water! Oh, deary deary me, what am I going to wear now for the church outing?"

"Now don't you upset yourself," said Pat. "Let me see what I can do. You know, they often wrap these things in plastic bags. The water may not have got into it at all."

"Well, then . . . how are we going to get it out?" said Dorothy.

"Has your Bill still got that fishing-rod his Aunt Ada sent him the Christmas before last?" said Pat.

"Yes, I think so," said Dorothy. "I think it's in the garage."

"Quick," said Pat. "See if you can find it."

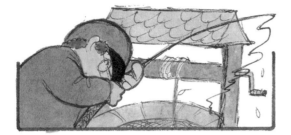

It didn't take long to find the fishing-rod. "Now," said Pat, "it's a long time since I did any fishing, but this should be easier than catching a trout. Here we go . . ."

Pat lowered the hook down the well. He could just see the parcel, lying in the muddy water. Luckily, one corner was poking out of the water. Pat dangled the hook by the parcel. He swung the line, trying to get the hook to catch in the string round the parcel. Missed! Missed again! It wasn't easy.

There, he almost had it. Try again. Yes, it's caught. Pull it up; slowly, slowly. It's coming.

Yes, it's coming; it's half way up, now, at least half way. Oh! It's fallen off the hook! Try again. It's fallen off again. Try yet again. It's on this time. Is it? Yes, it's coming! Careful, now, Pat. Slowly does it.

Pat wound the line in, so very carefully and slowly. The rod was bending with the weight, but the parcel was coming up out of the well. Got it! It was out.

Now, what would the dress be like inside the parcel? Pat shook as much water out of it as he could, then they took it into the kitchen, and put it in the sink. Water oozed and dribbled out of it. It was muddy and green with slime. How could the dress be all right inside that mess? Well, they could only hope for the best. Dorothy brought her scissors, and cut the string. Pat pulled off the soggy paper.

"What's this?" said Pat. "It doesn't feel like a dress. It's hard and . . ."

There was a box inside the paper, then some more packing, then . . . "That's a funny dress," said Pat. Then he began to laugh.

"It's nothing to laugh about," said Dorothy, "when . . . oh . . . oh!" She began to laugh with Pat.

What do you think was in the parcel?

A wet and muddy dress? No, not at all. It was a pair of wellingtons! Yes, wellingtons! Green, rubbery, wellingtons.

Whatever had happened? Had Pat brought the wrong parcel?

They were laughing so much, that it was five minutes before they could talk about it. Pat had to sit down and wipe his eyes with his hanky, he was laughing so much. Jess came to see what was going on, and walked out with his tail in the air, to show what he thought of them.

When they stopped laughing, Dorothy said, "I know . . . they must be Alf's wellingtons. He ordered some new wellingtons from the catalogue, but I forgot all about it. All the orders come with my name on, because it's my catalogue. I thought it must be my dress, because I've been waiting for it. Oh, dear, I haven't laughed so much for a long time!"

"Well, that's a piece of luck," said Pat; "muddy water won't harm a pair of wellingtons."

"Yes," said Dorothy," but I can't go on the church-outing in Alf's wellingtons, can I?"

There was another parcel for Dorothy Thompson the next day. This time, she put it on the kitchen table whilst she signed for it. This time, it was her new dress. It was dry, and clean, and tidy; just as it should be. It was a perfect fit, and it was just what she wanted. She wore it on the church outing, and everyone admired it.

Postman Pat's Breakdown

Postman Pat was driving along, singing a song to Jess, when the engine of his van began to make strange noises. It went splutter, pop, bang; splutter, whizz, squeak; fizz, buzz, rattle; or something rather like that. Pat stopped singing, and looked worried.

"Oh, dear," he said, "that sounds bad. We can't do with having a breakdown with all these letters to deliver. Come on, don't stop."

But the van wasn't listening. It began to go more slowly, no matter how hard Pat pressed his foot down. It began to go along in jerks, stopping and starting again. The engine began to cut out. Then, it gave a last cough, backfired with a loud bang that frightened the sheep, and stopped. Pat pressed the starter. There was a whirring sound, but the engine was dead. They were stuck.

"Now what are we going to do?" said Pat. "We haven't delivered a single letter."

Jess thought it was a good chance to get out and hunt for mice and rabbits along the hedge. Pat opened the bonnet, and looked at the engine. It looked just the way it always looked. He looked at the dip-stick. The oil was all right. He made sure there were no loose wires. He poked about for a while, then tried the starter again. It was no good. The engine had definitely decided to take a holiday. Pat looked up and down the road. All was quiet. They were a long way from any farms or houses.

"Someone's sure to come along, sooner or later," said Pat. He sat in the van and read his Pencaster Gazette.

After some time, Pat heard the ting-a-ling of a bicycle bell, and a whirring of wheels and pedals. Then he saw Miss Hubbard's hat sailing along above the hedge. She came round the corner, and almost ran into the van.

"Good gracious, Pat!" she said. "Whatever are you doing sitting here? Are there no letters today?"

Pat told her about his breakdown. She had to look at his engine. "Hm, it sounds as though you've blown a gasket," she said, "or else your big-end's gone. I once had a Riley that did that, in the middle of nowhere. You'll need a tow. I'll pop in at the Pottages, and see if Peter Fogg's about. Won't be long."

"Just a minute," said Pat. "I think I have some letters for you." He rummaged in his bag, and brought out three letters and a small parcel.

"Lovely. Thanks, Pat. Bye!" And off she went.

Whilst Pat was waiting, the milk-tanker came along. It was George Lancaster's cousin, Tim, driving it. He couldn't get past Pat's van. He had to stop, and help Pat to push the van into the side of the road, to make room.

"Hang on, a minute," said Pat. "There's a letter for George, and a card and a pools-coupon for you."

"Thanks," said Tim. "Cheers!"

Jess came back, with his fur all ruffled up, and with twigs and leaves tangled in it.

"I think I've found a new way to deliver letters," said Pat. "If we sit here long enough, everyone will come past; I'll just give them their letters as they pass by. It would save a lot of petrol, and you could hunt mice all day, Jess."

Pat read another page of the paper, then there was the sound of a tractor coming along the road. It was Peter Fogg, complete with tow-rope.

"Well, I'm glad to see you," said Pat. "Here we are; three letters, a magazine, your tax-form, and an advert for soap-powder. Oh, yes, and a broken-down van. I'm sorry to bother you . . ."

"Don't mention it," said Peter, "it's no bother at all. Let's get it out of the road."

Peter soon had the rope hitched up, and it didn't take long to tow Pat to Greendale Farm.

"We'll just push it in the barn, and I'll have a look at it," said Peter, "while you have a cup of tea."

Mrs. Pottage had the tea ready for Pat. He brought his bag of post in with him, as he had a lot of letters for the Pottage family, and two parcels, too. Peter came in with bad news.

"You'll need a new engine," he said.

"Oh dear," said Pat, "that means getting it towed in to Pencaster. I expect the Post Office will lend me a spare till it's mended."

"But what will you do about today's post?" said Mrs. Pottage. "You could have borrowed Herbert's Land-Rover, but he's gone off in it to buy some sheep."

"I'm just going to stand at the road-side, till everybody comes past," said Pat, "but it might take a long time."

"I know," said Mrs. Pottage, "you can borrow my bike. It only needs the tyres pumping up, and it'll be fine."

A little while later, Pat set out again, on Mrs. Pottage's bike. Jess sat in the basket at the front, and the bag of letters was tied on the carrier at the back. It was hard work pedalling up the hills, and Jess was cold in the basket. Oh, how they both longed for their warm van!

The bike jolted along the bumpy roads, and as they went along it seemed to get more bumpy and more jolty. When they stopped at the church, Pat saw why; the front wheel had a slow puncture, and it was quite flat by now.

"I'll just pump it up," said Pat. Then he saw that there was no pump on the bike. Peter had pumped it up with the van's foot-pump.

"Now what?" said Pat. "I wonder if the Reverend has a pump?"

Pat had a lot of letters for the Reverend Timms, and this made his bag much lighter.

"I'm sorry, Pat," said the Reverend, "I haven't got a pump. I always use the one at the garage in Pencaster; but I can give you a lift in my car – I have to go and see Ted about repairing the organ."

"That's very kind of you," said Pat.

It was quite a long job, getting the Reverend's car out. It was a very old Morris Minor. There was something wrong with the gears, and it wouldn't go backwards, so they had to push it out of the garage.

Then the Reverend couldn't find the key, until he remembered that he had hidden it under a vase of tulips in the vestry. Then it wouldn't start. Pat had to push it until they came to a hill, then he had to jump in quickly, and it started at last, with a roar, and clouds of blue smoke. Pat was on his way again, and Jess was much warmer, curled up on the back seat.

Ted was surprised to see Pat arriving with the Reverend, but pleased to have his letters, even if they were so very late. Pat told the story of his breakdown. As they were talking there was the sound of an engine coming up the road. Ted ran outside to stop whoever it was.

"Come on, Pat!" he shouted. "It's Alf with his trailer. He can give you a lift up to Thompson Ground."

So off went Pat and Jess again. Jolting and jouncing on Alf's trailer this time. I don't know what had been on Alf's trailer that morning, but it was very smelly. When they arrived at Thompson Ground, Dorothy was cross with Alf, and said he should have given Jess and Pat a clean piece of sacking to sit on. Never mind, Pat delivered more letters and parcels, and his bag was still lighter.

"Now, where is your next call, Pat?" said Dorothy.

"Granny Dryden," said Pat.

"Well that's a good way," said Alf. "Too far to walk, really."

"Well . . . I wonder?" said Dorothy. "I wonder if Pat could ride our pony? Miss Hubbard lives near Granny Dryden, and she has a stable. You could leave it there if you can get another lift home."

Pat wasn't so sure about this idea. He hadn't been on a pony for years and years, and Jess had never been on one.

"She's a good, quiet, creature," said Dorothy. "You'll be all right with our Lizzie."

Pat decided he would give it a try. He had never missed delivering the post yet, not once, and he hoped to win the Postman of the Year competition, in the Post Office newspaper. Yes, he would have a try. So, with a clip-clop of hooves, Pat set out again, up the steep road from Thompson Ground. Jess was tucked into his coat, out of the way.

All went well, until Pat decided to take a short cut to Granny Dryden's cottage. "There's no need to keep to the road on a horse," said Pat. "It will be much quicker if we go across the fields."

So Pat left the road, and set out across the field. Lizzie was a good and quiet horse, true enough, but Dorothy had not thought to tell Pat that she was scared of crossing streams. She had thought he would stay on the road. So, when they came to a stream, Lizzie would not cross it. She walked sideways, and backwards, and round in circles, but she would not cross the water. No matter how Pat asked her, or pulled at the reins, or patted her neck, she still would not cross the water.

Then, with all this turning and stepping up and down at the edge of the water, Lizzie put her foot in a rabbit hole. This gave her a fright, so that she reared up, tipping Pat, and Jess, and the bag of letters, all into the water, with a great splash! Pat struggled to hold the letters out of the water, and Lizzie ran off back to Thompson Ground. Jess hung on to Pat's shoulder with all his claws, to keep his paws dry. Pat was wet and muddy. What a mess! Luckily, the water was only a few inches deep, but it was very very cold. Pat sloshed out, and up the hill to Granny Dryden's cottage.

There was a shiny red Sierra standing outside Granny Dryden's cottage.

"That looks like Dr. Gilbertson's car," said Pat to Jess, as they squelched up to the door.

"Good gracious me, Pat, have you been for a swim?" said Granny Dryden, when she opened the door. "You've picked a cold day for it. You should wait till summer."

"Atishoooooooooo!" said Pat.

"Into that bathroom with you," said Dr. Gilbertson, "and get those wet clothes off before you catch your death of cold. We'll find you something dry to put on. You'd better get into a hot bath while you're about it."

But what could they find for Pat to wear, at Granny Dryden's house? Jess was soon all right. He gave himself a good wash, then sat by Granny Dryden's warm fire to dry out. But what about Pat? Granny Dryden opened her wardrobe, and rummaged through her drawers, but there was nothing that Pat could wear.

"We can't send him walking his rounds in a dress," said Dr. Gilbertson. "The only thing we can do is to wrap him in some blankets."

So they warmed some spare blankets in front of the fire, and handed them into the bathroom to Pat. He came out looking like a Roman in a film! Granny Dryden laughed so much, that Dr. Gilbertson said he had done her much more good than all her bottles of medicine.

The letters were only a little damp. There were quite a few for the two ladies, and the bag was getting almost empty. Pat sorted out the remaining letters on the table.

"I'm calling at all those places on my rounds," said Dr. Gilbertson, "so you can ride with me. It'll do my patients good to see you; they need a good laugh. We'd better be on our way. Goodbye, Mrs. Dryden. I'll see you next week."

Pat and Dr. Gilbertson were on their way. It was just as the doctor had said. Pat made such a comical sight, wrapped up in his blankets, that everyone they visited felt much better afterwards.

"You can come with me every day, if you like," said Dr. Gilbertson. "I think I'll put you on my list of medicines. Only, if you make everyone better, there'll be no work for me to do."

The next day, the Post Office said Pat could use another van until his own was mended, and he wore his spare uniform. Even though he didn't look funny now, he still cheered people up when he called with their letters and parcels, and stopped for a sup, and a chat, and a joke, and to swap all the news of the valley.

Postman Pat
On The Run

"Now, then," said Pat, one Thursday morning. "Has my new uniform come, yet?"

Pat had had his old uniform for a long, long time and it was very shabby. He had ordered a new one and had been waiting weeks and weeks for it to come.

"No, it hasn't," said Mrs. Goggins, looking at the label on a parcel, "but there are some new people for you, at Lane Head. They're Mr. and Mrs. Bagenal, and they have a lot of letters, and a large parcel."

"Oh," said Pat, "I'll have to carry that parcel half a mile; the road stops before it gets to Lane Head. They must have had a right time moving in; carrying their tables, and beds, and chairs, and everything, up there. I hope that parcel isn't too heavy."

"It's not too bad," said Mrs. Goggins.

Lane Head was near the end of Pat's round, so his bag was almost empty when he got there. It only had the post for Mr. and Mrs. Bagenal in it. He left the van at the end of the road, leaving Jess asleep in his basket. Then he set out to walk the rest of the way. As he climbed up the hilly field towards the house, he saw some white creatures in the far corner. He didn't take any notice of them until he was in the middle of the field, far away from any fence. Then he saw that the creatures were goats, and they were not tied up, the way goats usually are. They came running to Pat.

"Hello, then, Billy," said Pat, to the first one. "What friendly animals they are," he thought. Then, he saw the billy-goat put its head down, so that its sharp horns pointed at him. It stamped its feet, then ran at Pat.

"Help!" Pat shouted. "Help!"

Pat ran as fast as he could, with his bag swinging and banging on his legs, and getting in his way. He ran for the fence, but before he got to it, he felt the goat butting him from behind.

"Oh! Ow! Help!" Pat yelled, then he was at the fence. He jumped over, but caught his trousers on the barbed wire, and ripped a big hole in them. What a mess he was in!

When he reached the cottage, Mrs. Bagenal came to the door with a smile, and a, "Good morning, postman!"

Her smile soon disappeared when she saw his torn trousers, and he told her how it had happened.

"Oh, my goodness, I am sorry that happened," said Mrs. Bagenal, "but, you see, they aren't our goats at all. We're new here, and they've chased us, too. We go the long way round, now."

"Well, I haven't time to go the long way round," said Pat, "so I'll have to see if I can cure them of chasing people."

"You can't go home like that," said Mrs. Bagenal. "Let's see if we can patch you up."

She took him inside, and found a tin of safety-pins in a drawer. "Here we are, now, we can patch you up with these."

She pinned Pat's trousers together with safety-pins, all down the leg.

"Now you're not going back through that field, are you?" she said, when Pat had given her the parcel and letters.

"Oh, don't you worry," said Pat. "I have an idea for teaching that billy-goat a lesson."

Pat walked to the middle of the field. He held his empty bag ready, with its mouth open. He waited for the goat to charge at him.

"Come on, Billy, come on, I'm ready for you this time," Pat said to the goat.

The goat put its head down, pointed its horns at Pat, and charged. Pat stood still, holding the bag open. When it was almost touching him, he quickly popped the bag over its head, and pushed it down over its horns. The goat shook its head from side to side. It was puzzled. Why had everything gone dark and stuffy? Why couldn't it see anything? It bleated sadly. It shook and shook its head, but it could not shake the bag off. It tried to walk away from Pat, but it walked in a circle, and fell over its own legs. Oh dear, it was in a muddle.

"Well, now, have you learnt your lesson?" said Pat. "Can I have my bag back, yet?"

He pulled the bag off. The goat shook itself, and glared at Pat. It lowered its head and charged again! Look out, Pat! Pat was ready for it. He popped the bag over its head again. This time, he left it on longer.

The goat was getting quite dizzy, trying to shake it off. Pat took the bag off. All the time, the nanny-goat was quietly eating the grass, some distance away. She took no part in the game at all. The billy-goat looked dizzily at Pat; but, all the same, it lowered its head and charged again.

"Three times for luck," said Pat, popping the bag over its head again. He was getting very good at this, and the goat was getting worse and worse. Pat left the bag on a good long time, until the goat was so muddled that it had to sit down. He took the bag off. The goat gave him a wobbly look. It got unsteadily to its feet, and walked away. It stood with its back to Pat, pretending he wasn't there. Pat walked away, watching the goat all the time. It took no notice of him. It nibbled at the grass. Pat walked back to his van.

"You missed a good show," said Pat to Jess. "Pat the famous goat-fighter." Jess had been dreaming about rabbits. He didn't think he'd missed anything.

Pat called at the post-office. He told Mrs. Goggins about the goats, and showed her his torn trousers.

"You're in luck," said Mrs. Goggins, "because your new uniform came after you'd left this morning."

"My goodness, that is lucky," said Pat. "If it had come yesterday, I'd have had it on today, and it would have been torn, instead of the old one."

Pat took his new uniform home in its parcel, and tried it on. It looked very smart; so the day ended happily, after all.

"I hope there's no post for Mr. and Mrs. Bagenal to-morrow," said Pat, "but I think I'll take a spare empty bag with me, just in case I need it."

Pat Bakes a Cake

Sara and Julian were going off to Wooler for a week, to see Gran. There was a school holiday, and the weather wasn't too bad now, so it was a good time to go. Besides, they hadn't seen Gran for months and months. Pat saw them off at Pencaster station, very early in the morning.

Sara had left all kinds of nice things in the fridge, for Pat's dinners; but, Pat thought to himself, "I'll have a nice surprise ready, for when they come back."

Later that day, when he had finished delivering the post, Pat went to the village post-office. This time, he went to the grocery part of the counter. He bought some flour, margarine, sugar, eggs, icing- sugar, cherries, and dried fruit.

"Hum," said Mrs. Goggins, "it sounds as though your Sara's making a cake."

"Oh, no," said Pat. "They've gone to Wooler for the week. I'm making a cake. It's to be a surprise for when they come back."

"Do you often bake cakes, Pat?"

"No, I've never made one before," said Pat. "But I've got a good book from the mobile-library, that tells you how to do it. The book says it's easy. Won't Sara be pleased?"

"I hope so," said Mrs. Goggins.

Pat set to work that evening. He set everything out on the kitchen table, with the library-book propped open at the page headed – **"Fruit Cake"** – ready to begin. He read aloud from the book.

"Two hundred and fifty grams of flour."

He noticed that there were two kinds of flour – plain and self-raising. "Well, it's a plain cake," said Pat, "so I'll use plain flour."

He got the scales out and began to pour the flour into the bowl. He noticed that the dial on the scales was marked in ounces; it said not a word about grams.

"Hm, I wonder how many ounces there are in two hundred and fifty grams? It sounds a lot to me. I'll just have to guess."

He weighed out twenty-five ounces of flour, and read from the book again. *"Place flour and salt in bowl, and rub in the margarine."*

It was all in grams again, so he put a good dollop of margarine in the bowl, and shook the salt-cellar over it for a while.

"What's all this? *Rub in the margarine?* How on earth do you do that?"

He rubbed the piece of margarine about on the flour, but all it did was to puff flour up into his face. He simply buried the margarine in the flour, in the end.

"Add sugar and fruit, and beat the eggs and milk together. Mix everything together until it is soft."

It was still in grams, so he had to guess how much sugar and how much fruit to put in. Well, Sara always seemed to guess when she made cakes, and hers were always delicious. He mixed it as well as he could, but it seemed very lumpy.

"Place in a six-inch tin and bake in a moderate oven, for one-and-a-quarter hours."

He couldn't find a ruler to measure the tins, so he used the first one he found which did look rather big. Then . . .

"What is a *moderate* oven?" said Pat.

He looked at the back of the book, he looked at the front of the book, he looked all through the book, but it didn't say anywhere what it meant by a moderate oven. So he lit the oven, and twirled the knob round to number seven. "Seven for luck," he said. "It's my lucky number, always."

He popped the cake in the oven and closed the door.

He looked at his watch.

"Now if we go to watch television, Jess, the cake will be ready after the news."

Jess settled down by the fire. Pat settled down in his armchair. The fire was warm. Quite soon Jess's eyes began to close. Quite soon, Jess was fast asleep.

Pat watched a play on television. It was a boring play. Quite soon, Pat's eyes began to close. Quite soon, Pat was fast asleep.

Pat had a dream. He was being attacked by a tiger in India. It was trying to eat his leg. He could feel its sharp claws pulling at him. Pat woke up, with a jump. Jess was clawing at his trouser-leg, and there was a smokey smell coming from the kitchen. Pat jumped up, and ran to the kitchen. He opened the oven. Clouds of smoke came puffing out, and oh, what a smell! Pat turned the oven off. He put the big oven-gloves on his hands, and felt in the middle of the smoke for the cake. He found it. He brought it out and dropped it in the sink.

When the smoke cleared, Pat saw a cindery mess in the bottom of the tin. It did not look at all like a cake. When Pat tried to put it in the rubbish-bin, he found that the cake would not come out of the tin. He had to throw tin, and cake, and all, away.

"Never mind, Jess," said Pat. "We have a week before they come back. There's time to have another try."

When Pat went again, the next day, to buy flour, and sugar, and raisins, and cherries, and eggs and dried fruit, Mrs Goggins said, "Goodness, me, Pat, are you making another cake?"

"No," said Pat. "Well, yes, I am in a way. The first one went wrong. I'm having another try."

"Better luck, second time round," said Mrs. Goggins.

When Pat called at Greendale farm, Mrs. Pottage was busy making a cake. "What's all this about *rub in the margarine*," said Pat. "It doesn't tell you how to do it in my book."

"That's easy," said Mrs. Pottage. "Look, you just cut the margarine into small pieces, and rub it between your fingers, until it mixes with the flour."

Pat watched Mrs. Pottage's fingers closely. "Now I see," he said, smiling.

When Pat called on Dorothy Thompson, she was just putting the oven on.

"What's all this about *bake in a moderate oven*," said Pat. "It doesn't tell you in my cookery book."

"Gas Mark 4," said Dorothy. "They expect you to know that, of course."

Pat made a note in the back of his diary.

"Thanks," he said. "I wish I'd known that last night."

When Pat called on Miss Hubbard, she was making home-made wine. She was weighing out fruit and sugar.

"Do you know anything about these here grams they have in the cookery book these days," said Pat.

"I stick to ounces," said Miss Hubbard. "I'll have no truck with these new-fangled grams."

"The trouble is," said Pat, "I'm trying to make a cake from a library-book, and it's all in grams. I got in a proper muddle."

"Cake?" said Miss Hubbard. "Library-book? What a lot of rubbish. Look, here's my old mother's recipe-book. Turn to page twenty; there's a lovely recipe for fruit-cake there. Copy that down, and you won't go wrong."

"Thanks," said Pat. He wrote it in the back of his diary.

When Pat called on Ted Glen, he told him all about his cake, and what a mess he'd made of it.

"I've heard about it," said Ted. "News travels fast in Greendale. I think everybody knows about your cake."

"The trouble is," said Pat, "I've spoilt the tin as well as the cake, and Mrs. Goggins doesn't sell cake-tins."

"Don't worry," said Ted. "I'll make you one. I've been wanting something to try my new welder on. Call in, after you've finished your letters, and it'll be ready for you."

"Thanks, Ted. You're a marvel."

When Pat called on Granny Dryden, she was putting the icing on a birthday cake, for Katy and Tom Pottage. She had put the icing in a bag, with a hole in the corner. She was squeezing the bag so that the icing came out and wrote itself on the cake. It made patterns and words. Pat watched her.

"That's clever," said Pat "I think I'll try that."

Pat collected his new cake-tin from Ted on his way home. It was a rather strange cake-tin. It looked as though it had started life as something quite different; part of a car, or a washing-machine, perhaps.

"It's not like the cake-tins in the shops," said Ted. "None of this non-stick nonsense; but it'll do the job, O.K., if you give it a good greasing."

Pat looked at a tin of motor-grease, on a shelf. Ted laughed.

"Not with that! You have to get some butter on a piece of grease-proof paper, and rub it round the tin, inside. It stops the cake from sticking to the tin. You'll never get it out, if you don't do that."

"There's a lot to learn, about making cakes," said Pat. "I never knew there was so much to it. Thanks, Ted. Cheerio!"

Pat had another try at making his cake, that evening. He did all the things that his friends had told him. He set the alarm-clock to tell him when the cake would be ready. Jess went off to the Pottages' barn hunting mice, until it was all over. He thought it would be safer there. When Pat took the cake out of the oven, there was no smell of burning; there was a lovely smell of newly baked cake, just as there was when Sara made one. It came out of the tin perfectly, and it looked lovely.

All Greendale was waiting, the next day, to hear about Pat's cake. The news was good, but it still had to be iced, and, as Dr. Gilbertson said, "We won't know if it's a success until Sara comes home."

The next day, Pat started on the icing. The first batch of icing was too thin. When Pat put it on the cake, it slowly ran down the sides, on to the table. The second batch was too thick; it wouldn't come out of the icing-bag. The third batch was just right. Pat wrote, "WELCOME HOME," in pink icing, and left it to set.

When Sara and Julian came home, they were pleased to see a cake waiting for them. They all had a slice, and it was delicious.

"I didn't know you could make cakes," said Sara; "What a lovely surprise! Did it take long?"

"No," said Pat. "Only a few days."

Sara thought that sounded a long time, just for making one cake; but she was enjoying it so much that she didn't say so.

The next day, Sara found the remains of her cake-tin in the dustbin. I think it was a good thing that Pat, at the moment, was at the far end of Greendale, delivering letters. But he had a long story to tell when he came home.